PICTURE PUZZLES

Jenny Tyler
Illustrated and designed by
Graham Round

Contents

Hints on solving picture puzzles

To solve most of the puzzles in this book all you need do is use your powers of observation carefully. First of all, make sure you read the question properly so that you know what you are supposed to be looking for. Then look closely at each picture, or part of the picture if it is a big one, until you find it. Don't give up too soon – you will often find things in the pictures that you didn't see at all when you first looked.

For the "spot the difference" kind of puzzle, look at part of one of the pictures and try to fix an image of it in your mind. Then look at the same part of the other picture and compare it with the picture in your mind.

There is a picture symbol, like this:

next to some of the puzzles. This means that a pencil and paper would be useful. For mazes, it is best to lay tracing paper over the top and follow the way through with a coloured pencil. If you make a mistake, you can throw the paper away and start again with a new piece.

For a few of the puzzles there is a clue on page 32. These have a picture symbol like this:

next to them. You will find the answers to all these picture puzzles on pages 26 to 32.

Cardboard train

This collection of boxes, rolls and corks was used to make a model of a train. Every single piece was used but nothing extra was added. Which of these models is the one that was built from this group of objects?

Match pictures and badges

Here are some boxes of pictures and some badges. What you have to do is find the badge which best fits the *group* of pictures in each box.

First choose a badge for the group of pictures in the BLUE box.

Next choose a badge for the group of things in the RED box.

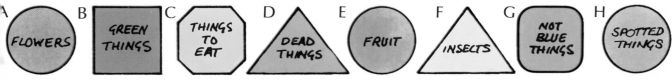

A FLOWERS B GREEN THINGS C THINGS TO EAT D DEAD THINGS E FRUIT F INSECTS G NOT BLUE THINGS H SPOTTED THINGS

Jigsaw pieces

Here are six jigsaw pieces which will fit together if you put them in the right order. Which piece goes next to which?

Which face is next

Here is a series of faces. Can you work out which of the faces in the row below should come next in the series?

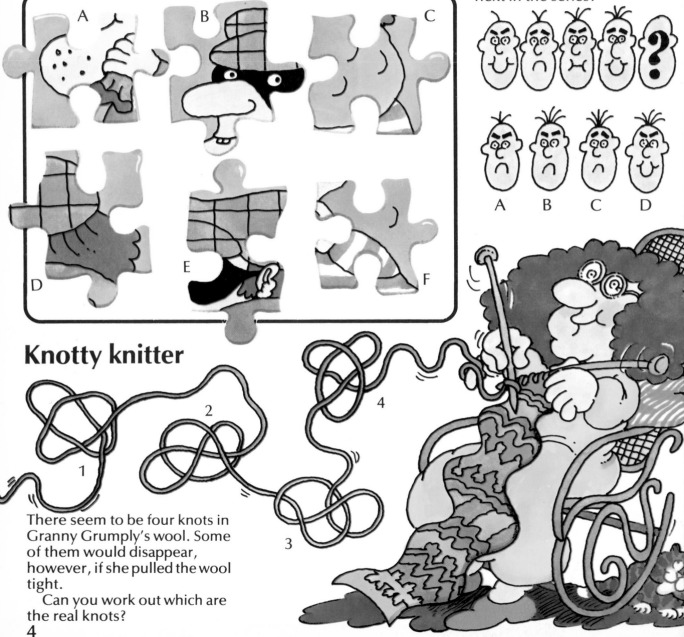

Knotty knitter

There seem to be four knots in Granny Grumply's wool. Some of them would disappear, however, if she pulled the wool tight.

Can you work out which are the real knots?

4

Which map?

Curly, Carrots, Fingers and Joe each tried to draw a map of where they live. Only one of them got the map right. Who was it?

CARROTS

JOE

FINGERS

CURLY

Tangled lines

Four inexperienced anglers went fishing together. Find out what each of them has caught.

1   2   3   4

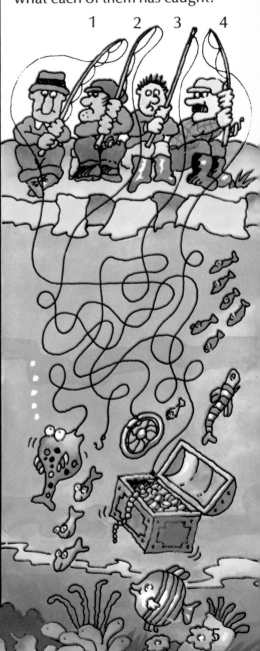

5

Mirror puzzle

Countess Crinklyface is putting on her make-up. Which of the four pictures below shows her face as she sees it in the mirror?

A

B

C

D

Three cats

Which of these cats is the biggest? Guess first, then measure to see if you were right.

Fake picture

The owner of this picture claims that it was painted over 300 years ago. But famous art historian, Art Y. Brush, says it is a fake because it is full of mistakes. How many mistakes can you find?

)) If you get stuck, look at the clue on page 32.

Mixed-up snapshots

Sammy cut his holiday snapshots into pieces and mixed them up. His Granny soon worked out which piece belonged to which snapshot. Can you?

Find the twin cats

Two of these cats are the same. The others are slightly different in some way. Can you find the twins?

1   2   3   4   5   6   7   8   9

Caught red-handed

Trapped in a beam of light, Light-fingered Pete is caught in the act of stealing the jewels. But there is something wrong with this picture. Can you work out what it is?

Easy chair

This chair was drawn in one continuous line, without the pen being removed from the page and without any part of the line being covered twice. Can you work out how?

You will need to trace this one.

Doodlesaur puzzle

Here are some Doodlesaurs.

Here are some creatures which are not Doodlesaurs.

Which of these creatures are Doodlesaurs?

1

2

3

4

9

What does the letter say?

This torn-up letter was found in a waste-paper basket.
Can you work out what it says?

Which cat comes next?

Which one of the cats numbered 1 to 4 below should come next in the row on top of the wall?

Dice problem

Which of the dice below could be made from this unfolded one?

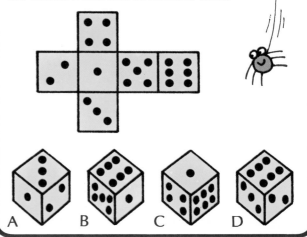

A   B   C   D

10

Mixed-up puppet

Can you sort out this puppet's strings?

A B C D E F G H

HEAD

NECK

LEFT HAND

LEFT KNEE

RIGHT HAND

LEFT FOOT

RIGHT KNEE

RIGHT FOOT

Which TV picture?

TV CAMERA

A television programme is being made about The Great Magico, a world famous magician.

Which of these pictures do you think the viewers will see on their screens?

A

B

C

D

11

Slug puzzle

Two umbrellas

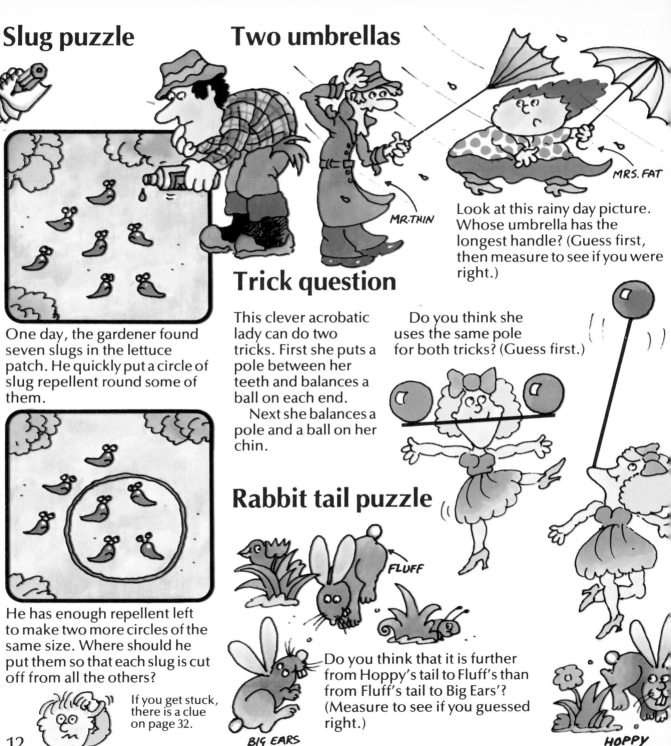

MR. THIN

MRS. FAT

Look at this rainy day picture. Whose umbrella has the longest handle? (Guess first, then measure to see if you were right.)

One day, the gardener found seven slugs in the lettuce patch. He quickly put a circle of slug repellent round some of them.

Trick question

This clever acrobatic lady can do two tricks. First she puts a pole between her teeth and balances a ball on each end.

Next she balances a pole and a ball on her chin.

Do you think she uses the same pole for both tricks? (Guess first.)

Rabbit tail puzzle

FLUFF

He has enough repellent left to make two more circles of the same size. Where should he put them so that each slug is cut off from all the others?

If you get stuck, there is a clue on page 32.

Do you think that it is further from Hoppy's tail to Fluff's than from Fluff's tail to Big Ears'? (Measure to see if you guessed right.)

BIG EARS

HOPPY

12

Party puzzle

Which of the six tables on the right is laid exactly like the one at the party mentioned below? Read the following information and work it out.

Jim said there was a big cake with pink icing and six chocolate drops on top. There was a plate of square sandwiches too. The table was covered with a red striped cloth.

Fred said there were triangular sandwiches. Next to these, on the right, there was a large red jelly.

Joan said the jelly was green and there were square chocolate biscuits.

Sue said she specially liked the little cakes with cherries on top. There were six of those. She thought the tablecloth had yellow spots on it.

Jack said the cake was covered with white icing. There were no chocolate biscuits and the sandwiches were horrible.

Jack later admitted that he had not told the truth and Joan said she had got confused with another party. The other three were right.

13

Mirror pictures

If you rest the edge of a mirror in a certain place on some pictures, you will see that the reflection in the mirror completes the picture, like this:

The place where you rest the mirror when this happens is called a "line of symmetry". Look at the pictures and work out (using a mirror if you like) which ones have a line of symmetry.

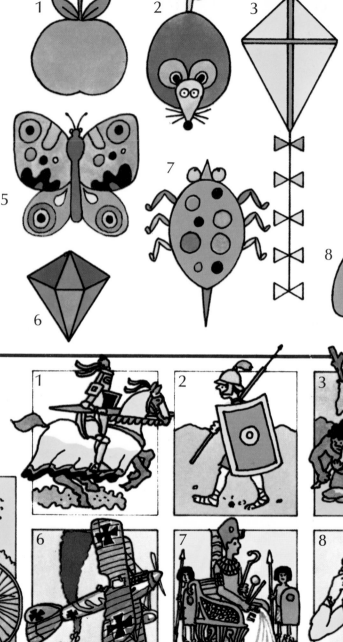

Time puzzle

These pictures show scenes from long ago. Can you sort them out into the order in which they happened?

14

Find the missing pieces

These pieces belong to the picture on the left. Which piece fits where?

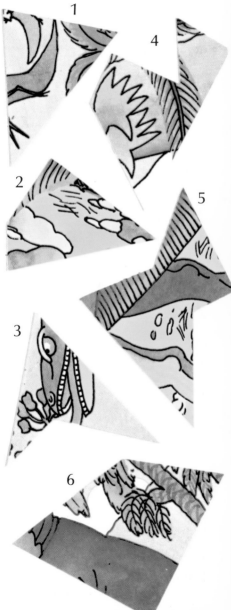

1

4

2

5

3

6

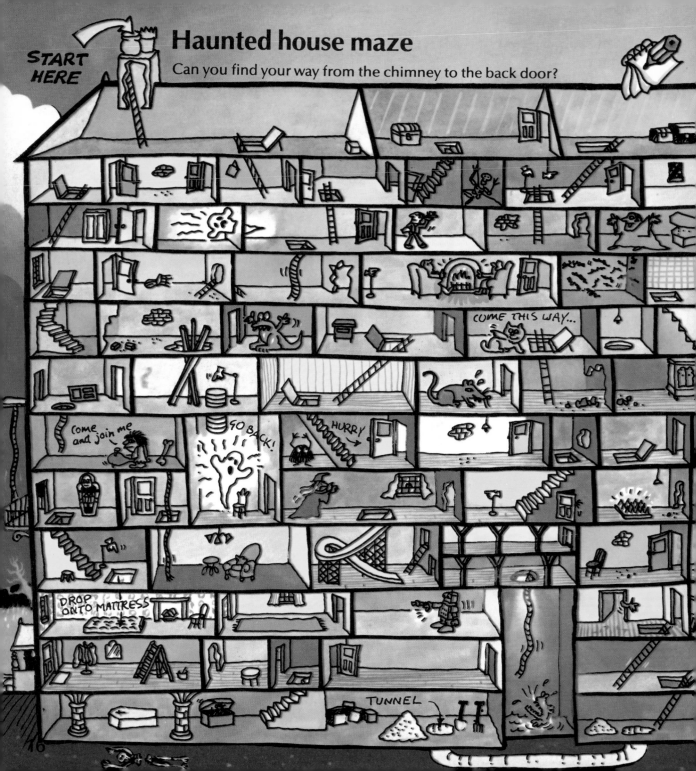

How many hiding places?

These two old ladies are really spies in disguise, but they quickly hid all their equipment when they heard you coming. Can you find all the places where they have hidden things?

Tangled group

Can you sort out whose guitar is plugged into each amplifier?

STRUMMER (RHYTHM GUITAR)

RED (BASS GUITAR)

PINKIE (SECOND LEAD GUITAR)

SPIDER (LEAD GUITAR)

A   B   C   D

Picture pairs

Each of these coloured shapes has something special in common with one of the others. Sort them out into twos and say what each pair has in common.

1

2

3

4

5

6

7

8

Odd picture

Which of these pictures is the odd one out and why?

1

2

3

4

5

19

Label the bag

Which of these labels best describes the contents of the bag at the bottom of the page?

A. Paper things

B. Red and blue things

C. Not round things

D. Not green things

E. Things to read

F. Things to eat

Spot the difference

These two pictures look the same at first sight, but when you look closely you will find that some things are different. There are, in fact, 20 differences between the pictures. See if you can find them all.

HENRY VIII

ELIZABETH I

NAPOLEON

LINCOLN

CLEOPATRA

20

Which cog?

Sue needed a new cog wheel for her bicycle. She knew it must have ten square teeth and a round hole in the centre. The man in the shop told her to sort through this box. Which one should she buy?

Where is the missing painting?

There has been a robbery at the Abstract Art Gallery. The Gallery officials are particularly upset because the painting was part of a famous and valuable sequence. The police have come to solve the crime, but unfortunately no-one at the Gallery can remember exactly what the painting looks like.

Can you tell them which of the paintings below is the stolen one?

If you get stuck, look up the clue on page 32.

1

2

3

4

Another odd picture

Which of these pictures is the odd one out and why?

A

B

C

D

E

Which house fits the plan?

This is a plan of the ground floor of a house. Can you work out which of these houses it belongs to?

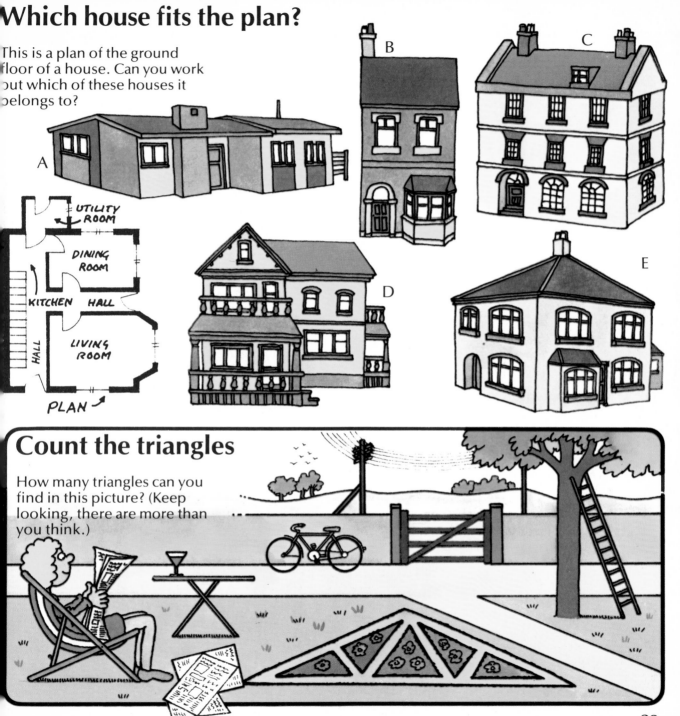

UTILITY ROOM

DINING ROOM

KITCHEN   HALL

HALL

LIVING ROOM

PLAN

A

B

C

D

E

Count the triangles

How many triangles can you find in this picture? (Keep looking, there are more than you think.)

Find the mistakes

There are 23 things wrong with this picture. Can you find out what they all are?

Find the odd shoe

These shoes all look the same, but one is slightly different from the others. Which one?

If you get stuck, there is a clue on page 32.

A B C D E F G H

Identibits puzzle

Which of these "identibits" belong to the face shown here?

Mixed-up story

This picture-strip story is all mixed up. Sort out the pictures and put them in the order in which they could have happened.

If you get stuck, look at the clue on page 32.

Answers

Page 3

Cardboard train

Model A was built from the collection of objects in the picture.

Match pictures and badges

GREEN THINGS is best for the blue box.

NOT BLUE THINGS is the best badge for the red box.

Page 4

Jigsaw pieces

Here is the completed jigsaw.

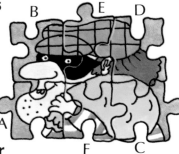

Knotty knitter

Knots 1 and 3 are real.

Which face is next?

Face B should come next in the row.

Page 5

Which map?

Fingers was the only one to draw the right map.

Tangled lines

Fisherman 1 caught nothing.
Fisherman 2 caught the box of treasure.
Fisherman 3 caught the wheel.
Fisherman 4 caught the fish.

Page 6

Mirror puzzle

Picture C shows what Countess Crinklyface sees in the mirror.

Three cats   They are all the same size.

Fake picture

There are 22 mistakes. Here they all are:

Page 8

Mixed-up snapshots

Here are the sorted out pictures.

Find the twin cats

Cats 2 and 6 are the twins.

Page 9

Caught red-handed

The shadow of Light-fingered Pete is pointing in the wrong direction – it should be pointing into the picture.

Easy chair

Follow the arrows on this picture to see how to draw the chair.

Doodlesaur puzzle

Creatures 2 and 4 are Doodlesaurs, 1 and 3 are not. Here is how you can tell:
The first three pictures tell you that Doodlesaurs have red eyes, straight tails, sometimes have spots and are blue or green.

Page 10

What does the letter say?

Here is the complete letter, so you can read what it says.

Which cat comes next?

Cat 4 should come next on the wall.

Dice puzzle

Dice A and D are the same as the unfolded one.

Page 11

Mixed-up puppet

String A goes to the puppet's head.
String B goes to the puppet's right hand.
String C goes to the puppet's left foot.
String D goes to the puppet's left knee.
String E goes to the puppet's left hand.
String F goes to the puppet's neck.
String G goes to the puppet's right foot.
String H goes to the puppet's right knee.

Which TV picture?

Picture B is the one the viewers will see.

Page 12

Slug puzzle

The picture above shows where the slug repellent circles should go.

Two umbrellas

Mr Thin's umbrella handle is the same length as Mrs Fat's.

Trick question

She can do both tricks with the same pole because it is the same length in both pictures.

Rabbit tail puzzle

The distance from Hoppy's tail to Fluff's is the same as that from Fluff's to Big Ears'.

Page 13

Party puzzle

Table 4 shows what there was to eat at the party.

Page 14

Mirror pictures

Pictures 1, 3, 4, 6 and 8 have a line of symmetry.

Time puzzle

The correct order for the pictures is:
4 (Dinosaur, which lived about 100 million years ago)
3 (Stone Age hunters, who lived about 1½ million years ago)
7 (Ancient Egyptian pharaoh, about 3½ thousand years ago)
2 (Ancient Roman soldier, who lived about 2,000 years ago)
1 (Medieval knight, who lived about 900 years ago)
8 (Elizabethan man, who lived about 400 years ago)
5 (Penny-farthing bicycle, which was in use about 100 years ago)
6 (Early aeroplane, in use about 60 years ago)

Page 15

Find the missing pieces

The pieces fit as follows:
piece 1 (B), piece 2 (E), piece 3 (A), piece 4 (D), piece 5 (F), piece 6 (C).

Page 16 Haunted house maze Here is the route through the house.

Page 18

How many hiding places?

The hiding places are ringed on the picture on the left. There are 21 of them altogether.

Page 19

Tangled group

Pinkie's guitar is plugged into D.
Spider's guitar is plugged into A.
Red's guitar is plugged into B.
Strummer's guitar is plugged into C.

Picture pairs

1 and 8 are a pair because they both have spots.
2 and 4 are a pair because they are both the same shape.

6 and 5 are a pair because they both have stripes.
3 and 7 are a pair because they are both the same colour.

Odd picture

Picture 4 is the odd one. it is the only back view. All the others show front views.

Page 20

Label the bag

Label D fits the bag best.

Spot the differences

The places where the two pictures are different are ringed in this picture. ▶

Page 21

Which cog?

Sue should buy cog 5.

Page 22

Where is the missing painting?

Picture 2 is the stolen one.

Another odd picture

Picture C is the odd one out – it is the only thing in the group which doesn't come in pairs.

Page 23

Which house fits the plan?

House E is the only one which fits.

Count the triangles

There are at least 31 triangles in the picture. You can see where they are on this picture. You may be able to find some more but remember they must be complete triangles.

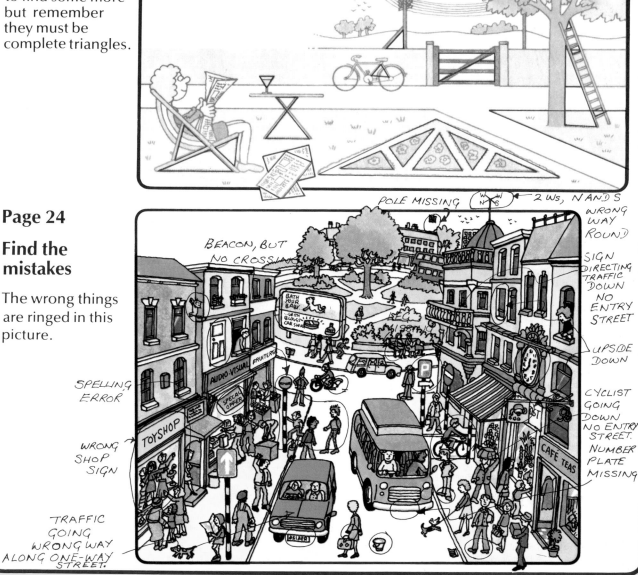

Page 24

Find the mistakes

The wrong things are ringed in this picture.

Find the odd shoe

Shoe F is the different one.

Page 25

Identibits puzzle

Pieces 2, 3, 4, 6, 9, 10 and 14 fit the face, the others don't.

Mixed-up story

The pictures should be in this order; 4, 2, 5, 1, 3.

First published in 1980 by
Usborne Publishing Ltd,
Usborne House, 83-85 Saffron Hill,
London EC1N 8RT, England.
Copyright © 1987, 1980 Usborne Publishing Ltd

The name Usborne and the device are
Trade Marks of Usborne Publishing Ltd.

Printed in Belgium

Clues

Page 6

Fake picture

There are 22 things wrong. See if you can find them all before looking at the answer.

Page 12

Slug puzzle

The picture shows where the second circle goes. Now see if you can work out the position of the third one.

Page 22

Where is the missing painting?

Notice that the picture is turned round each time and that the colours move round too, but always stay in the same order. Now have another look.

Page 24

Find the odd shoe

Look very very carefully at the laces.

Page 25

Mixed-up story

Notice how dirty the players are.